The Spotted Stones

The Spotted Stones

▾

by Silvio A. Bedini
pictures by Richard Erdoes

Pantheon Books

Text Copyright © 1978 by Silvio A. Bedini. Illustrations Copyright © 1978 by Richard
Erdoes. All rights reserved under International and Pan-American Copyright Conven-
tions. Published in the United States by Pantheon Books, a division of Random House,
Inc., New York, and simultaneously in Canada by Random House of Canada Limited,
Toronto. *Library of Congress Cataloging in Publication Data.* Bedini, Silvio A.   The
spotted stones. Summary: Two Italian monks who are imprisoned as spies while on a
pilgrimage invent a new game to pass the time in a dungeon. [1. Dominoes—
Fiction. 2. Games—Fiction]   I. Erdoes, Richard.   II.   Title.   PZ7.B38193Sp
[Fic]   78-3283   ISBN 0-394-83573-5   ISBN 0-394-93573-X   lib.   bdg.
Manufactured in the United States of America.   10   9   8   7   6   5   4   3   2   1

To Gena

The ancient monastery in Southern Italy was alive with excitement. The morning had begun like any other day with monks rising at dawn, attending mass in the chapel followed by a simple breakfast in the refectory. But then there was a break in the normal routine. Instead of moving on to their individual tasks on the premises and the farm, the monks had gathered in the courtyard and were talking with each other in hushed but eager tones. For today two of their number were about to leave on a pilgrimage to a shrine in a distant province. It was far to the north, and no one from the monastery had ever visited it.

Brother Magro and Brother Grasso had made a pledge months before, and the Father Superior had finally approved their journey. The two monks had packed their few necessities and some food into knapsacks and now they waited impatiently for the Father Superior's blessing so that they could be gone.

Released at last with warm expressions of goodwill from their fellow monks, Magro and Grasso set forth through the great gate down the steep hill to the main highway. They made a strange pair as they walked together. Brother Magro was extremely tall and thin, with a sad face, and he was inclined to see life without humor. Brother Grasso was his complete opposite. Short and rotund, his round red face was generally merry and mirrored his warm disposition and optimistic outlook.

They hurried along the dusty road as the sun emerged over the horizon. It was spring, and the day was already warm with a slight

2

breeze. The countryside seemed more brilliant and green than they had ever known it. Months had passed since the last time they had left the monastery, and the outside world beckoned them.

The monks made steady progress during the first part of their journey. When they had finished the food and wine they had brought with them, they stopped at parish houses or at farms where they were fed and sheltered for the night. The days passed quickly as they moved through the province.

But then they reached a new and unfamiliar land. They had difficulty understanding the dialect of the region and lost their way.

"I wonder where we are?" queried Grasso as they were traveling on a steep mountainous road that seemed to have no ending. "This is the most desolate countryside I have ever seen!"

"True, we have not seen a farmhouse for miles," responded Magro. "Everything looks different, and it's getting late."

"We will have to find some place to spend the night soon," added Grasso, "besides which, I'm hungry!"

"You're always hungry," grumbled Magro, "but I agree we had better find shelter soon, or we shall have to sleep on the highway."

The sun was setting, and the silence all about them gave them an uneasy feeling as they continued their steep walk. The road climbed steadily upward, winding around what appeared to be a large mountain. Finally, they saw the first signs of life.

"Look!" called out Grasso. "Up there—a castle! Right on the top of the mountain!"

"Let's walk a little faster," urged Magro. "Maybe we can reach it before dark."

"Faster? I can't walk faster!" protested Grasso. "With your long legs, you take one step to my every two. I'm worn out!"

Tired and disgruntled and bickering, the monks continued on their way, hastening as much as they were able. As they approached the castle, the scene opened up to give them a wide view of the region. The two monks paused to rest a moment as they surveyed their surroundings.

The land dropped off abruptly, and far below they could see a small village perched on the sloping countryside, as well as several isolated farms in the distance. The highway along which they had traveled appeared to have been carved out of the rocky mountainside, with ledges projecting along its sides.

The road before them led to a drawbridge over a deep, wide moat which encircled the castle. The great fortress of stone, which towered immediately above their heads, looked ominous and forbidding. As they gazed up at the structure in awe, they saw that the figures walking along the parapets were armed guards.

"It doesn't look very friendly, does it?" commented Grasso. "Perhaps we should turn around and go back the way we came."

"Not at this hour," responded Magro. "But maybe we can avoid the castle and make our way down to that little village. I noticed a church there among the houses."

"Let's do that," agreed Grasso. "Those soldiers up there would probably sooner give us battle than food. The villagers will be more friendly."

6

They immediately began to retrace their steps along the steep road, seeking a way to reach the village. They had made some progress over the ledges to the grassy slope below them when they were stopped by an authoritative voice.

"Halt! Who goes there?"

The monks froze in their footsteps and remained silent as they listened to the sound of approaching steps.

"Let's run!" whispered Grasso. "We must not let them catch us here!"

"Why? We've done nothing wrong," answered Magro, somewhat uncertainly. "But it's too late anyway! Here they come!" At that moment two soldiers turned the corner of the ledges, and they found themselves face to face.

"Who are you?" thundered one of the soldiers. "What are you doing here?"

The monks understood the words with difficulty because of the unfamiliar dialect, but there was no misunderstanding the tone or the intent of the questioning.

"We are two monks on a pilgrimage," explained Magro carefully, as Grasso stood shaking beside him. "We have come from a monastery far to the south. We seek food and shelter."

"Food and shelter indeed! Then what are you doing off the road?"

"We were trying to reach the church in the village where we could spend the night," said Magro.

"A likely story!" snorted the soldier. "We'll soon learn what you are doing here. Forward, march!"

"Where are you taking us?" quavered Grasso.

"To the prince," replied the soldier gruffly, as he hurried them before him at a brisk pace. In a short time they found themselves over the drawbridge and ushered roughly into a large room filled with soldiers and courtiers. At the far end of the room a tall stern old man sat upon a throne.

"What have we here?" he rumbled fiercely as they appeared. "Who are these foreigners?"

"They are spies, Your Highness," answered the soldier. "We caught them on the slopes below the castle."

"Spies, are they?" The prince looked at the monks closely. "Sorry looking spies, I'd say! But they'll be even sorrier when we get through with them!"

"What shall be done with them, Sire?" inquired the soldier.

"Into the dungeon with them for now," ordered the prince. "We'll question them and find out what they are up to. We'll teach them not to spy!"

The monks were herded roughly along the corridors of the castle and down a narrow, winding stairway until they reached the basement level. Their captors unlocked a great barred door and pushed them into a dungeon. The door clanked shut behind them, and they heard the key turn in the great lock. They looked about them in bewilderment.

The room was lighted by a lone candle, but moonlight filtered through a small window high in one wall. There was only the simplest furniture. A crude table with two stools stood in the center of the room. Two beds made of wooden boards and covered with straw were placed along one wall. The floor was earthen.

The smell of damp soil mingled with wet straw. Other unpleasant odors betrayed the presence of mice, or worse.

"What shall we do now?" mourned Grasso, sitting down wearily. "No supper, and I have never been so hungry!"

"That's the least of our problems, I would say," retorted Magro. "Do you realize that we might be in this jail for years? They might even kill us! We must find a way out of here—and soon!''

"Find a way out?" Grasso went to the door and looked out through the spyhole. "No chance! We wouldn't be here at all if you hadn't tried to find a short cut to the village!"

"So now it's all my fault!" countered Magro. "We had better try to get some sleep. Nothing will happen until tomorrow."

The monks stretched uncomfortably and uneasily on their hard beds. But tired from their long walk, they quickly fell into a sound sleep.

The prisoners were awakened by the thin shaft of sunlight which came through their small window. They arose and said their prayers and then waited impatiently for some sign of life outside their cell. It was not until late in the morning that a guard arrived with a simple breakfast. The monks ate ravenously.

"Well, at least we got a good night's sleep, and now we have eaten," commented Magro, as he got up from the table. "We are ready now for whatever happens next."

"Eaten?" Grasso complained. "You call that a meal? I could eat two more loaves of bread all by myself!"

The day passed quietly, interrupted only when their meager meals were brought to them at noon and at sunset. No one came to question them, as they had expected. When several days had passed in the same way, the monks contemplated their future with growing concern.

"What are we going to do?" asked Grasso anxiously. "We have been prisoners for almost a week, and I'll bet they have forgotten we are even here!"

Still nothing happened, and the days lengthened into weeks. By climbing upon the table, which they moved under the window, and then standing on one another's back, they were able to glimpse the distant countryside. Each time they looked, their freedom seemed all the more unattainable. They explored every corner and crevice of their dungeon again and again, but they could find no way of escape. Then one day Magro noticed that Grasso was concentrating on a small area of the floor where he appeared to be scratching in the earth.

"What are you doing?" Magro called. "Counting stones? That's a silly way to pass the time! What will you do after you have counted them all?"

"Count them all over again, of course!" snapped Grasso. "Look! Here's another spotted pebble." Magro ignored him, and some time later Grasso called out again.

"Here's another! This one has four spots!"

Magro stretched himself out full length on his bed and closed his eyes. Counting stones, indeed! They had better think of a way to get to see the prince so that they could talk their way out of there.

Grasso continued to scour the dungeon floor diligently in search of other pebbles marked with spots. What had begun as a diversion to pass the endless hours of boredom had now become a serious preoccupation and a challenge.

In the days that followed Grasso was successful in collecting a substantial number of flat bone-white stones marked with spots. They seemed to be a native rock that resembled marble. Some of the stones were heavily spotted all over while others were marked, as if by design, with spots only on one side falling in neat patterns. Grasso now attempted to find the pebbles with different groupings of spots. He dug deeper into the packed surface of the floor.

One morning the guards, watching through the spyhole in the door, noticed this unusual activity.

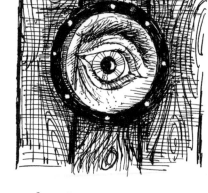

"What do you think that is all about?" one of the guards asked another.

"Who knows?" the other responded. "He has probably just gone stir crazy! It happens."

"But look over there," the first guard pointed. "He's been digging. Maybe he is trying to dig a tunnel to escape under the wall!"

"You're right. We had better keep a closer eye on them from now on," the second guard agreed, "and report their suspicious actions to the captain of the guard, just in case!"

Meanwhile, Grasso had collected an impressive pile of flat spotted pebbles, and he was seated at the table moving them around. Suddenly he called out excitedly.

"Now we have pebbles with spots on one side from one to six! And here are some with even more spots!"

"Great," commented Magro sourly. "And now what do we do?"

"I have been trying to work out a game," explained Grasso. "A game that two can play,

17

and it will help to pass the time. These are the best pebbles. See? There are twenty-four of them, and to each player we give four of those that have spots from one to six."

"All right then, show me how we play," agreed Magro. He was bored, and even the most simple activity would be a welcome change in the long day.

Grasso explained that, according to his scheme, they should start with the pebbles

18

heaped in the middle of the table, with their marked surfaces turned downward. Each player was to take six of the stones, look at them but not reveal their spots to his opponent. The player having a stone with six spots would start the game by placing it on the table.

"I have one with six spots," said Magro, "so I will start. I just place it face up on the table?"

"That's right," Grasso agreed. "Now I have to match it. Since I do not have a stone with six spots in my pile, I have to take another stone from the heap until I find one. The idea is that the player who first uses up all his stones is the winner."

So saying, Grasso took more pebbles from the heap, one by one, until at last he found one with six spots, and he placed it next to the one on the table. To continue the game, Magro took another stone from his store and placed it also on the table. It had three spots, and Grasso readily found one to match it. Magro then offered a stone with five spots, and Grasso matched it, and so the game proceeded.

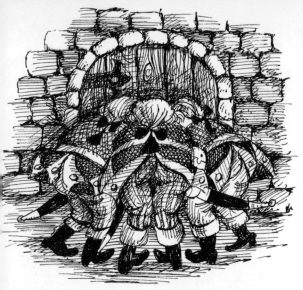

The time passed quickly, and the monks enjoyed the minor challenge that the game offered. Again and again they played, while the guards took turns watching through the spyhole.

"What are they up to now?" one would ask the other suspiciously.

"Up to no good, that's for certain," would be the answer. "We had better keep a sharp eye on them!"

As the two prisoners played on, one game after another, their captors became increasingly concerned.

"This is serious business," commented the captain of the guard. "Something is going on in there, and we don't know what it is. I must inform the chamberlain before it is too late!" He went upstairs to seek out the master of the prince's household.

"Stones?" inquired the chamberlain with

annoyance. "What could they possibly do with stones?"

"But, Sire," insisted the captain, "I think they are planning an escape! They are spending hours at whatever their scheme is!"

"Very well, I will have to go and see for myself," said the chamberlain ungraciously. "Take me to the dungeon!"

The guards before the cell door drew back
respectfully as the chamberlain appeared and
made his way to the spyhole. He observed
intently and became increasingly puzzled as
he watched.

"There are spots on those stones," he commented, turning to the captain of the guards. "It may be some form of secret writing. You are right!"

"They may be planning to escape, and the messages may be intended for someone outside the castle," answered the chamberlain. "Yes, that must be it!"

"Double the castle guard immediately!" ordered the captain. "We must not take any chances. We'll have to keep a closer watch on them than before."

The monks, although fully aware that their activity had caused increasing concern outside, continued their game. But the game became boring after a while, so they devised ways to improve it. They discovered that by selecting stones that had no more than six spots they could make it more interesting. Then they added four pebbles with no spots at all and assigned each other a total of six stones. But even with these variations the game was not challenging enough, and they continued to try new ways to improve it.

"I have an idea!" exclaimed Magro at last. "As it stands now, we are matching pebble for pebble, and there is no link between the sets of numbers. But if each stone has two groups of spots, the game would have continuation."

"That's a splendid idea," said Grasso, "but I don't think we can find stones that are marked in that manner."

"But I am thinking that we can mark the stones ourselves!" said Magro, and he lowered his voice as he told his plan to Grasso. The monks knew that they had an audience at the spyhole, and they were beginning to take pleasure in confusing the guards.

That evening after supper, the two prisoners laid out the stones on the table and set to work. Using small, sharp pebbles they began by scratching the surface of each stone. Then with a straw from their bedding which they dipped into the wine they had saved from their meal, they traced a line across each stone and made dots on either side of it. When one pebble was done it was put aside to dry, and they worked on another.

The guards, watching through the spyhole, became more and more excited.

"Send for the captain," whispered one. "They are up to something new."

The captain agreed that the monks' activity was indeed suspicious. Beyond that he did not know what to make of it, so he summoned the chamberlain.

Meanwhile the monks went on quietly with their project. Their work went slowly. The stones were difficult to mark because the wine would run and smear. But stone by stone they perfected their technique, and the pile of marked stones mounted. Outside their cell the watchers could hardly contain themselves as their curiosity mounted.

"They have gone mad!" pronounced one of the guards in a low voice.

"No, they are preparing secret messages!" retorted the captain. "Clever! Very clever! They are spies! I knew that when we captured them!"

"Can you see what they are writing on those stones?" asked the chamberlain, quietly.

"Yes, they are drawing lines and dots," answered the guard.

"Lines and dots . . ." mused the chamberlain. "Obviously it is some sort of secret writing. It is time to inform the prince. He must see this for himself!"

The captain dispatched one of the guards to tell the prince, while the others clambered for a view through the spyhole. The monks, aware of being watched, were greatly amused. They were playing with the newly marked

stones and seemed to greatly enjoy the new version of their game when the prince arrived. The prince watched for a time, then returned to his chambers, accompanied by the chamberlain and the captain of the guards. It was time for a council. After discussing the suspicious activity they had all observed, they agreed that the prisoners must be spies and that they

should be put to death—but not until the prince could learn more about their plot.

"They must not be permitted to get in touch with anyone from the outside," the prince warned, "for it may be that our land is in danger from one of our enemies!"

In their dungeon Magro and Grasso continued their game, but they now got less pleasure from matching the spotted stones than they did from listening to the movement and whisperings of the guards.

"I wish we could confuse them even more," commented Grasso, in a low voice.

"I have it!" responded Magro. "Let's say something that will make them think we are speaking a strange language. I am sure none of them know Latin. Let's pick a phrase we can use instead of 'I win!'"

"Splendid!" agreed Grasso. "Why don't we use a nice sounding phrase from one of our prayers?"

"Good idea! Now let's see . . ." Magro mused. "How about *Dixit Dominus Domino meo?*"

"That's great," said Grasso. *"Dixit Dominus Domino meo!* It's just right."

The monks continued their game, calling out the Latin phrase each time that one of them won, making certain that the guards heard it clearly. The guards were indeed listening.

"There—they said it again!" said one. "These monks can't be Italians from another province. Now we know. They are speaking a foreign language!"

"There's no more doubt about it," agreed another, "they are really spies."

"I must go and hear for myself," said the
prince, when he was told of this new develop-
ment. "Lead me to the dungeon!"

He saw the monks seated as usual, deep in
concentration, with the stones arranged before
them in a symmetrical pattern. Then Magro
moved his last stone.

"Dixit Dominus Domino meo!" The tall
monk called out the words clearly and trium-
phantly.

"Quick! Unlock the door and let me in,"
ordered the prince. "I must find out for myself
what is going on in there!"

"On your feet!" shouted the captain, as he

led the prince into the dungeon. Roughly, the guards began to pull the monks from their stools.

"Wait! Wait!" called the prince. "Let them be. I want to see what they were doing with the stones. Go on!" he ordered the monks. "Keep on with what you were doing." He watched as the prisoners made ready for another game. He followed every move they made.

"What is this all about?" he asked at last. "What are you doing? Composing a secret message, no doubt!"

The monks were amused, but when they saw the prince's expression they prepared to explain their game.

"Your Highness," responded Magro respectfully, "this is a game we have invented to pass the time while awaiting your pleasure. Come, see for yourself!"

"A game?" inquired the prince. "What do you call this game?"

"It has no name, Sire," said Magro.

"Would you like to see how we play it?" volunteered Grasso.

"Yes, let me see how it is done," said the prince, taking Grasso's place at the table. He wore a quizzical look, but he listened patiently as the monks took turns explaining the game and how they had developed it. Then the prince played a game with Magro. The tall monk winning, shouted, *"Dixit Dominus Domino meo!"*

The prince was startled. "What did you say? What is the meaning of those words?" he demanded.

"It's a phrase from a Latin prayer," Grasso explained with a smile. "It means 'The Lord said to my Lord . . .'"

"*Dixit Dominus Domino meo,*" repeated the prince. "Hmmm. It has a lovely sound, but it's too long. Why not have the winner just call out *Domino?*"

The monks promptly agreed, and they prepared the spotted stones for another game.

"No, not here!" the prince decided. "It is too damp and cold! We will move upstairs to my chambers, where we can play in comfort."

So the prince and the monks moved to the throne room, where the prince had a table set up for the game. They played all day and into the night, game after game. The monks could hardly keep their eyes open as the hours passed, but the prince was relentless in his insistence that they play again and again. At last he, too, was exhausted, and he arranged for the monks to be moved into royal guest rooms near his own.

The prince was up and about early the next morning and insisted that the monks join him as soon as possible to play the game. Magro and Grasso grumbled. They were not ready to leave their soft beds but they had enjoyed a

34

pleasant rest, and the breakfast exceeded even
Grasso's expectations.

Again they spent the whole day playing
their game with the prince, while the chamberlain, captain of the guards, and members of the
court stood around them and watched with
growing interest. But when the monks pro-
posed that the courtiers be taught the game too,
the prince ignored their suggestion.

Every day thereafter was the same. The

prince now had his own set of spotted stones, prepared for him by his craftsman. Every morning he summoned Magro and Grasso even before they had finished breakfast, and all day they took turns playing with him. He seemed never to tire of the game. But the monks became restless and irritable and impatient to be on their way. However, they were afraid to ask the prince for permission to leave. But one morning when Magro felt he could not bear to play another game, he summoned up enough courage to speak to the prince.

"We greatly enjoy playing with Your Highness," he began, "but after all, we are your prisoners, and . . ."

"Nonsense!" snorted the prince. "Forget all about that! You are no longer my prisoners—you are my guests! You need but to ask for what you want in the castle, and you are totally free to move about!"

"That's wonderful news, Sire," crowed Grasso. "In that case, we must resume our journey right away!"

"Not so fast, Brother Grasso!" snapped the

prince. "Leave? Who said anything about leaving? I said you were free to do as you like *in* the castle. How can I play *Domino* if you leave? Come, let's have another game!"

The monks were in despair. That night after the prince had retired, they talked together in their room.

"Why did I do it?" cried out Grasso, beating his head. "If I hadn't invented the silly game, we would not have this problem!"

"True," said Magro, "but if you hadn't invented the game we would probably still be in that stinking dungeon, or maybe shot as spies." They spent the rest of the night moaning and reproaching themselves until, exhausted, they fell asleep. The next morning Grasso awoke with an idea which he explained in great secrecy to Magro.

That morning when the chamberlain and the other courtiers had gathered around the table where Grasso was playing with the prince, Magro quietly whispered in the chamberlain's ear that perhaps he too might like to learn the game. The chamberlain, who had become more and more interested in watching his master play, promptly consented and slipped away with Magro to a corner of the throne room where they could play undisturbed. Not many days passed before the chamberlain was teaching it to the prime minister who taught it to the generals who taught it to the captain of the guard who taught it to the cook who taught it to the servants. Soon every member of the prince's household had learned to play the game.

"So far so good," commented Magro to his companion one night. "We have quite a few people playing the game. Now we have another problem."

"What's that?" asked Grasso.

"Well, there are only two sets of spotted stones," Magro replied, "and we need more sets."

The next morning, while Grasso was playing with the prince, Magro quietly slipped away to find the craftsman who had made the prince's set.

The craftsman agreed to make the pieces if Magro, in turn, would teach him how to play the game. And since the spotted stones were hard to find, he would cut the pieces out of bones left from the kitchen.

"Dotted bones!" That's wonderful," said Grasso, when he heard the news.

And it turned out that so many craftsmen wanted to learn the prince's game of Domino, as they called it, that soon the two monks had a great many sets of bone pieces which they gave

to the courtiers,

 the servants,

and even to the guards.

Soon everyone was playing Domino. The prince's minsters were not attending to affairs of state, the courtiers were not courting, the servants were not serving, the guards were not guarding. The castle became a shambles. And in the village, people who had been taught by the craftsmen were spending their time playing instead of plowing the fields.

The prince was so absorbed with his playing that he never noticed when the chamberlain took over the game from Grasso. (It was the chamberlain's great ambition to play a game with the prince.)

"This is it," whispered Magro. "Let's go!"

They stole to the kitchen for food, which they hid under their robes.

Then unnoticed by all, they tiptoed through the castle and out the door

and made their way down to the main gate,
where the guards were so deeply immersed

in their game that they did not even look up as the monks walked by them.

The two monks passed through the gate and
over the drawbridge, leaving the castle behind.

Their steps quickened, and soon they were running down the mountainside and on their way to the shrine that was, after all, their destination.

The weather was sunny and warm, and the days and the distance passed quickly.

For food and lodging they stopped at farm-
houses and villages along the way.

They were well received, for they repaid their hospitality by teaching their hosts the game of Domino. And that is how the game first became known and how it became so popular throughout Italy and the rest of the world.

Historical Note

The origin of the game of dominoes is obscure. It is known, however, that it was played in one form in China several centuries ago and was introduced into Europe through Italy during the 18th century. How the game came to Italy, or whether it was independently re-invented there, is not known. At the time, Italy was divided into small city-states ruled independently by princes and dukes, and wars between the city-states were frequent.

According to tradition, the game of dominoes spread quickly throughout Italy and from there to France and Germany. It found its way to England by the end of the 18th century, and from there the game came to the United States early in the 19th century.

Throughout this period, the game of dominoes was played with flat rectangular pieces of bone inscribed with dividing lines and with varying numbers of spots. It was not until about 1840 that these domino pieces, or "tiles" as they were called, were modified by gluing the bone strip to a backing made of ebony and fastened with small brass pins. Later the tiles were reproduced in inexpensive sets made of wood, and in modern times, of plastic. The game of dominoes has remained one of the most popular of all games, and it continues to be played all over the world.

Silvio A. Bedini combines his interests in history, science and literature as the Deputy Director of the National Museum of History and Technology at the Smithsonian Institution. He is the author of three adult books—*Thinkers and Tinkers:* Early Men of Science, *The Life of Benjamin Banneker,* and *Moon, Man's Greatest Adventure* (with W. Von Braun and F. Whipple)—and he has numerous and fascinating other books in the works. He was born in Ridgefield, Connecticut and now lives in Washington, D.C.

Richard Erdoes an artist, photographer and writer, has been closely linked with the Indian civil rights movement ever since a *Life* assignment took him west in 1953. He is the author of several books, including *The Rain Dance People, The Sun Dance People,* and *The Sound of Flutes,* and is also a well-known illustrator. He was born in Vienna and now divides his time between New York City and Santa Fe, New Mexico.